NEVERMORE
NIGHTMARES

SINISTER SOCIETY

This book is for entertainment purposes only.

Printed in Oliver Springs, Tennessee, United States of America

Library of Congress Control Number:

Description: Crimson Cult Media, 2025 | Audience. Adult. | Summary: Horror Anthology

Ebook ISBN: 979-8-89467-033-1

Hardcover ISBN: 979-8-89467-034-8

Paperback ISBN: 979-8-89467-032-4

CONTENTS

NEVERMORE NIGHTMARES

The Sinister Society

CRIMSON CULT MEDIA

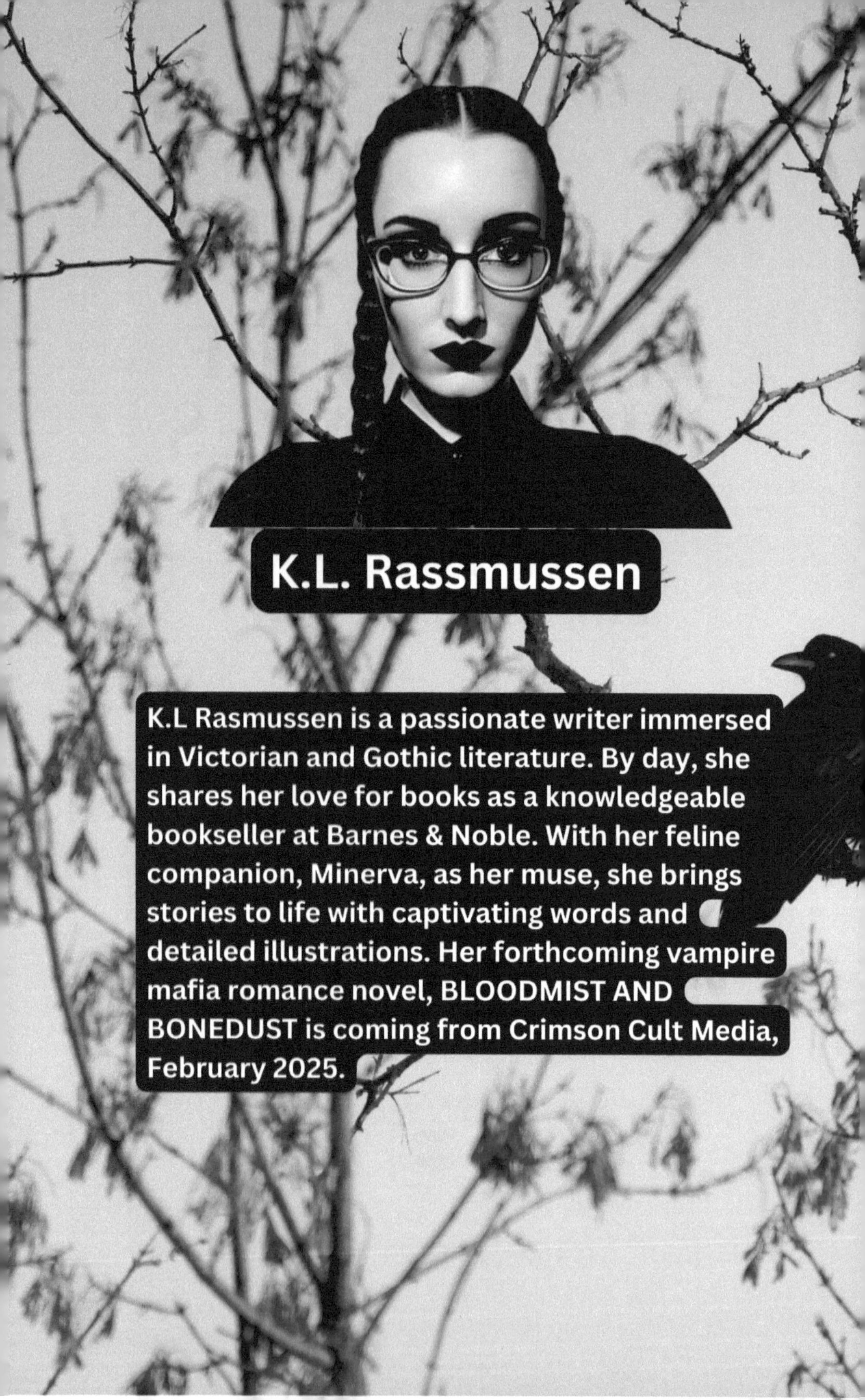

K.L. Rassmussen

K.L Rasmussen is a passionate writer immersed in Victorian and Gothic literature. By day, she shares her love for books as a knowledgeable bookseller at Barnes & Noble. With her feline companion, Minerva, as her muse, she brings stories to life with captivating words and detailed illustrations. Her forthcoming vampire mafia romance novel, BLOODMIST AND BONEDUST is coming from Crimson Cult Media, February 2025.

RAVENOUS, NEVERMORE

K.L. Rasmussen

Lament raps on my bedroom window, followed by the gloomy presence of this grim winter night. The shadows that haunt my window sill flit like bats, dancing and playing out my sorrows like a macabre ballet for only the night sky to see. I lay awake and watch them, hoping that exhaustion will soon overwhelm me and that I forget all notions of mourning my loss.

I toss and turn to no avail. Alas, my eyes are peeled open like grapes, wide awake and looking for that shadow of doubt in the darkness beyond my bed. It will come back, I think. I look to the window and feel haunted by the reflection of the cathedral's steeple hanging midair in the sky beyond. The light bouncing from the window to the bathroom mirror and the back of the mirror over the spare bed make the perfect projection of my disdain.

"Why did you take her from me?" I seethe, grieving into the sheets.

I rebuke all intentions of getting sleep tonight, as my loneliness and grief gnaw away at me. My mind buzzes awake the moment sleep creeps in, only to be stirred awake once more. The horrid drafts of the old family house creep in through the thin blanket, draping my shivering and lonely corpse.

How I miss her, I whisper to myself. Speaking to the dead does nothing to bring them back. Even pretending that her small body is wrapped around mine after I sought her womanhood with violent claims and bites of love, I cannot create an illusion of warmth in this cryptic room—the room in which we shared once. Only but a month ago her warm, contagious giggle echoed in these halls, and now its absence haunts me.

Silence fills the hollow space between my organs, where her love once flowed loudly in my veins, a vital part of my existence. Her corpse is now cold and silent. No longer laughing. The joy and beauty that once resided within her now wither away with the rest of her. No one to keep that flame of simple kindness of her memory alive. Except for me. In some way, we all keep each other alive.

And then the dreaded tapping begins its rhythmic tune. Coming from somewhere above, I do not know. I'd tear the house apart just to find its source. What a blessing in disguise that would be. To waste this place away to nothing, the bitter reflection of what is inside of me.

Tap! Tap-tap! Tap!

I pull the pillow over my head with force, but beyond the fibers, the tapping is still wrought on.

The screams of the young man I once was, now buried behind in my past, emanate from these walls. I never thought I'd find myself under this roof once more. But my great aunt Francis insisted upon my coming to stay after the horrid ordeal. To get away and gain some perspective on my life as a widower. Lucky for me, Francis had about ten years or more experience since her Joseph died.

I returned expecting to find fragments of the boy who once sought refuge here. Yet all that I find is a man who is letting the death of his fiancé slice him open more and more as each day passes, like the sharp blade of a pendulum sinking deeper with each swing of time ticking on without her.

The same dread and pain that comes with the tapping. The dreadful tapping. Surely it couldn't be my dear aunt Francis making this tormenting racket. And I'd have a lot of nerve to yell at an old woman for such a simple annoyance.

However, my exhausted body torments me to rise from the thin sheets and venture out to find the source of this torturous racket.

The dark corridor dissipates into the darkness leading to Francis's bedroom, a room I dare not cross the threshold of. It was her only request that her bedroom not be gazed upon by any other man than her late husband. I respected him, so I respected that request and had thought to turn around and abandon this silly little quest. I stop in my tracks when the violent tapping grows louder.

Stronger.

Closer.

Is it above me directly on the roof, or in the foundations of the home?

The home was built by Aunt Francis' husband Joseph himself. Guided by the influences of Japanese architecture and design, Joe built Francis a multibillion-dollar designer home. Warmth spread to my toes for the first time as the brick-laid floor emanated the heat from below.

A godsend to this house. Warm feet, perfect for the frigid winters. However, the efforts to get that have been astronomical.

The house was not made for this new heating system, but it was the latest and would be an effort to minimize our carbon footprint. Aunt Francis was easy to persuade, as she had no clear understanding of modern technology. But it was new and better, so it had to go in the house. As an amateur architect, taking in Joseph's footsteps as he was a surrogate father to me, it was deemed fit by Aunt Fanny that I oversaw the reconstruction of the floor and made sure none of her and Joseph's prized possessions disappeared from the home as workers wandered in and out of the elegant home.

I gladly took on that role. I was the man of the house now, and the man couldn't go raving mad at the sound of simple pecking—that won't *fucking* stop.

I'd go out into the main living room, but it is a wreck of construction and Francis is a light sleeper—she will hear me if I were to step in the gaping hole in the floor, which makes me confident that this dreadful pecking is a figment of my deranged imagination.

Francis would have been chasing whatever was out there away from her beloved garden. Any of the small animals that manage to clamor up the historic hill would find refuge in the Eden-like garden that Francis carefully designed.

I turn away from the window, the lights from the city now blaring in and making it unbearably bright. The curtains are dismally nailed to the wall, rendering them a piece of useless decor, something I will have to change once the flooring is done. One project at a time, with my grief already weighing heavy.

Most days I have a hard time staying awake, and most nights I lay in bed here, waiting for the incessant pecking. Even if I manage to fall into a restful slumber before the hour of three passes, I still find myself wide awake, as if an internal alarm wakes me just to ponder my lonesome existence.

Facing the emerald-painted wall, I embrace the darkness. The wall had built-in drawers that became a nice stash spot for some bud that I reserved for particularly difficult nights. Francis hasn't noticed my stock of plants that I have strategically placed down under the balcony in the space that meets the basement door. Francis hardly goes down there, and even if so, I don't think she'd have the heart to kill a plant.

Flowers are her passion. Having cultivated a reputation as the 'Flower Lady,' Francis found every moment of every day to show others the wonder of flowers. She would wander out onto the sidewalk and find passing families and stragglers to come to look at her garden. I've recently been putting a stop to that, as she could very easily invite someone nefarious who would gladly bury her among her beloved flowers before robbing us blind. I worry about Francis; while she's managed on her own for some time, there are moments when she starts to slip. I've found watering cans on the burning stove instead of a pot of water.

A few times I've found her wandering the streets toward the chapel to discuss the flower arrangements, only to be confused and lost just a few feet from the driveway.

Tap-tap-tap!

Ach! There it is again, and just when I thought it had ceased it's ruckus for the night. The noise is coming from above as if it haunts my part of the house exclusively. I have half the mind to find the ladder and crawl up there and destroy its creator.

I can't be much for good company these days. I am exhausted and lost in my grief. On the edge with all of the calls that were coming through for changes in construction and keeping Francis from setting the house on fire and running out into the street, the tapping is just the catalyst of madness. Keeping me awake to mourn the one person who made this life whole.

Lenore.

Tap-tap-tap!

If she were here, she'd be in the twin bed across the room, whispering to me in the middle of the night about how she, too, could never sleep comfortably on these lumpy mattresses. I would make the joke that we make use of the green foam arrangement blocks in the garage.

'It might straighten out that crooked back of yours,' she would giggle.

Tap-tap-tap!

I can feel it reverberating in that spot in my back that likes to pull if I stretch just in the wrong way. Looking up at the clerestory windows running alongside the wall, I see two dark, beady eyes peeking through the foliage climbing up the wall outside in the courtyard garden.

A raven croaking and clicking its beak at me, in observant mockery of my grief-ridden insomnia. Climbing the plants and tearing up the garden that Francis likes to water in the morning before her tea and hairdresser appointment. It tilts its head, beak ajar as if to say something, only to release a clicking noise before pecking the window.

At the very corner of the window, a faint crack begins to form. Oh, god. No.

I jump from my bed and dash out into the hall. Panic and rage surge through my body, and adrenaline floods my bloodstream. The front door is just a few feet away. I dash across the room—but to my dismal despair and failure to mark the construction zone properly—I lose my footing on a barrier marker and fall into the pit. I am met at the bottom with a lone hacksaw set aside, ready for use.

I lay in shock as warm blood pools at the wound, and I feel my limbs go numb with death, and yet my thoughts are not with the raven nor my life.

They're with her, or were.

Here I lie, ravenous for her love, nevermore.

David E. Anderson

David E. Anderson grew up in the '70s, loving Godzilla movies and the "Night Stalker" series, developing a love for horror early on. As a teenager, he immersed himself in the books by the likes of Stephen King, F. Paul Wilson and Dean Koontz, and wanted to try his hand at what they do so well. He wrote his first novel, "The Void," in his mid-teens, followed by six more—three of which he's self-published. Watch for news about his debut novel, SWEET DREAMS, coming spring 2025!

ECHOES OF LILITH

DAVID E. ANDERSON

I find myself in a shadowed quarter of the waterfront, an area that belongs to the fallen—prostitutes and the cads who barter for a fragment of their affections under Boston's gas streetlights.

The streetwalkers are a delight to me. Their willingness to follow a stranger wherever he may lead makes them vulnerable to what I have in mind. And even the most cautious of them succumb to my will in the end.

Oh, I do not kill them—at least, not usually. Though there is an unspeakable satisfaction in draining a body dry, it doesn't serve me well to leave a long trail of corpses in my wake. No, I am measured in my indulgence, taking nothing more than what's required to keep me satisfied for a few more nights.

But something about the woman I follow tonight—a woman I've never laid eyes on before—intrigues me. She hums as she walks the cobblestones, her voice lilting pleasantly through the chilly autumn air. The melody is familiar. I can't quite place it, but it gnaws at the edges of my memory.

Her hair is dark, and the gaslight reveals a reddish tint. A navy blue cloak is draped over her shoulders. Beneath, a yellow dress, faded but still clinging to its cheerful hue, gently sways as she walks to the tune issuing from her throat, her steps light, almost playful.

Her demeanor—unnaturally pleasant amidst the dreary waterfront—strikes me as a form of armor, protecting her psyche against the sordid life she lives. She fights a battle within her very soul, a struggle to preserve her true self.

Is it futile to imagine hope and optimism might emerge unscathed from a life that demands she sell her body to strangers nightly? Time will tell.

She stops to let a carriage pass, still humming as the driver rudely strikes his horse, cursing. The dreadful encounter is quickly forgotten, and she continues her stroll.

I quicken my pace, intending to catch up to her, to pose as a vice seeker and lure her into a solitary location. She will be mine tonight—this I have decided.

But as I draw near, her voice goes from humming to singing, and her words stop me cold in my tracks.

"I seek no more the fine and gay,
For each does but remind me

How swift the hours did pass away.

With the girl I left behind me."

It cannot be! She is long gone, a ghost of my mortal past. And yet, the voice that reaches my ears—I'd swear it is Lilith!

That very song once echoed through my heart, bright with joy and sweet with the promise of a love that transcends space and time. How many nights did I listen to that melody, the notes dancing in the air, sung by my ever-faithful Lilith?

It cannot be, yet here it is, undeniably seeping into my soul like a savage reminder of what I'd done to the love of my life.

I abandoned her in London two centuries ago, hoping to spare her from the curse that had befallen me. I fled into the night, forsaking my promise to meet Lilith at the altar. I feared what horrors I might bestow upon her if I remained by her side.

Yet guilt has followed me ever since, a specter that will not be silenced. What became of her, I cannot know. Did she find solace in another's arms? Bear the children she so desired? Did she enjoy a full and happy life, dying peacefully among those who loved her?

Or did my desertion cast her into an abyss of despair, resulting in a miserable and solitary end?

Could this woman before me actually be Lilith, risen from my memory to stand before me once more? Could she have traversed the ocean of time, as well as the actual ocean, to confront me with the weight of my betrayal?

No, I let the delusion wither and fade as if waking from a dream. Lilith surely passed on from this world over a century hence. While I have yet to see this woman's face, her hair is dark. It has a faint whisper of red, yes, but my lover's blazed like fire.

The woman turns, the side of her face briefly illuminated as she pauses to peruse a shop window. My breath catches. This woman bears Lilith's likeness. Her nose. Her chin. But her eyes are dim where Lilith's could light up a graveyard. Not my lost love, but perhaps a descendant?

As she continues her way along the cobblestones, I resolve to abandon the hunt. The hunger within me can wait another night. To feed from this woman, this enigmatic creature who has stirred my long-buried humanity, would now be unthinkable.

And yet, to turn away and seek the blood of another feels equally impossible. There is something about this situation, a sense of fate turning its eyes upon me, and I must see where this night leads.

She reaches a worn wooden door on a brick building and knocks, her shoulders sagging. My heart sinks as I recognize the place—it belongs to a man named Sutter, whose name is whispered in fear by many of Boston's ladies of the night.

The door opens, and he emerges with a bottle of rum in hand. His suspenders hang crookedly over his stained trousers, and his torn shirt, missing a couple of buttons, barely covers his bloated gut.

Sutter looks at the woman with disgust. "I 'ope you've done well by me tonight," he slurs, then rubs his mouth with the back of his hand.

"Oh, y-yes, sir," she says with a frantic nod. She holds out a pouch in a trembling hand, and he rips it from her grip.

He looks inside and grimaces. "Tha's all? Three measly clams?"

"Sir!" she shouts. "You said—"

He drops the coins into his pants pocket, then thrusts the empty pouch into her hand. "Get back out there, girl, before I bust yer jaw wide open! You ain't some virgin 'oo 'asn't a clue how to please a man, are ya?"

"No, sir! Of course not!" She steps back as if expecting to be struck, or perhaps just dodging the flying spittle accompanying his harsh words.

He holds up three fingers. "I'll be needing three more from you tonight, you 'ear me?"

"But I've been out for six hours already, sir, and—"

"Three more! Or..." He raises a tight fist, drawing back his elbow. The red bruises on his knuckles tell me this is a threat he has often carried out.

She backs away, holding up her hands in front of her. "Yes, sir."

"Ya worthless slag," he mumbles, then goes back inside, slamming the door.

She stands there facing the door, trying to put on a brave countenance, but the tears won't be held back for long.

I've felt little sympathy for humans since I turned, but my heart hurts for her. I imagine Lilith being in her position. Oh, with her family's money, she would never have stooped to selling herself, but this poor creature clearly doesn't have other options.

She collects herself, then turns, walking toward me. She takes a few steps before spotting me for the first time.

She pauses, her eyes lingering on my face, seeing my dark hair and sharp cheekbones. She puts on a smile and approaches, seeing no reason to avoid me. Women have often regarded me as attractive and approachable, and though the face I wear is unchanged by the centuries, I cannot help but see it now as a mask hiding the predator beneath.

I behold her clearly for the first time myself, and her resemblance to Lilith is uncanny. Not so exact as to call this woman a doppelganger, but were they not separated by two centuries and a vast ocean, one might likely have mistaken them for sisters.

"Hello, good sir," she says, a slight tremble in her voice betraying her attempt to be cheerful.

"Good evening," I say. "And who might you be?"

"My name is Ellen. And you are?"

"Drake," I say. "I couldn't help but see…" I point to Sutter's door.

"Oh," she says, and her face reddens. "My apologies." She forces a hollow laugh. "He's a bit drunk. He doesn't always act that way."

"I've heard different," I say.

Ellen grits her teeth. "I suppose, then, that you've discerned what I do for a living."

"In this part of town, this late at night?" I ask. "I'd be shocked if you were anything but. Perhaps I might be of help, though."

"How nice of you, Drake. Do you know of a place where we might be alone? If not—"

"No need for us to be alone," I say.

Delving into my pocket, I withdraw a handful of coins, the spoils of a poker game played in the shadowy recesses of a tavern the previous night. My preternatural senses make it easy to determine whether a player is bluffing or holding a winning hand, ensuring I never rise from such tables with pockets lighter than when I took my seat. From the coins I pluck three silver dollars, the bulk of my winnings, and press them into her palm. "This should keep Sutter off your back."

"Oh, thank you, sir! How kind!" Her smile blooms with sincerity. "So, where should we go to conclude this transaction?"

"There is no transaction," I say. "It's a gift, my dear Ellen, to help you out in your unfortunate situation."

"You are far too generous, sir!" she says.

"Go warm yourself somewhere and give those to Sutter in an hour or two, so that he might think you spent your time earning them."

Her face falls as she stares at the coins in her hand. "I can't," she says.

"Why not?"

"You don't understand," she says with a sigh of resignation. "Never once have I earned six dollars in a single night. And if I do, he'll expect it from me every night. Oh, if I return to him tonight empty-handed, he'll beat me; of that, there's no doubt. But if I bring him six and fail to meet that mark every night henceforth, he'll beat me every night henceforth. I've seen it with my own eyes, I have—girls left broken, one sent half-dead to the hospital."

"I see." I can't help but frown, knowing I am the architect of her despair.

"Oh, dear," she murmurs, lifting a hand to cover her face. "I do apologize, sir. You're only trying to help a poor lass, and I'm making you feel sorry for your efforts. My problems are not your problems. Thank you for the offer of help, but I'm a big girl and can handle myself, I can." She holds out the silver dollars as if she expects me to retrieve them.

I reach out and wrap my hand around hers, closing it on the coins. "They're yours, Ellen. Do what you will with them, but do not return to Sutter's door within the hour. Understood?"

"Maybe he'll have passed out by then and will leave me alone," she says with a laugh, glancing back.

"He may well be," I say. *Or worse.*

"Well, goodnight, sir. And thank you for caring." With that, she scurries off.

I watch her leave, then walk up and pound on Sutter's door.

The door creaks open, and Sutter's bloodshot eyes narrow at the sight of me. "Oo the 'ell are you?" he asks, then raises the bottle to his cracked lips and takes a swig.

"My name is Drake. May I come in?"

He belches. "Whadda you want?"

I want to drain the life out of him for the misery he inflicts upon Ellen and the others, but first things first. "May I come in?"

He huffs. "I asked what the 'ell you want!"

"I implore you to invite me in," I say through clenched teeth, my voice laced with the fierce edge of command as I summon my will.

The barrier that keeps me from crossing one's threshold uninvited is a mystery even to me. But the required permission can be wrung from a man unwillingly.

His expression falters, his resistance crumbling. "Fine, come in," he mutters, stumbling back, and I proceed within.

The room reeks of sweat, rum, and despair. Three women recline on threadbare cushions, their expressions hollow and haunted, their faces adorned with makeup too crude to fully hide evidence of the violence that had been visited upon them.

I command them to leave with a wave of my hand, using my powers to make it more than a simple request, and they obey.

Sutter watches them go, his bravado faltering as the front door closes behind the last woman. "Awright, what the 'ell's this about?"

I step closer, letting him see the icy darkness in my eyes. "It's about justice."

He chuckles drunkenly. "You don't look like no lawman. What are ya, some kind of vigilante?"

"No. Something far worse." I part my jaws, baring my elongated fangs and hissing like a serpent.

His eyes widen, his ruddy complexion fading to gray. "Christ!" he gasps, and his legs wobble.

He throws a punch, a clumsy swing fueled by fear. I catch his wrist in mid-air, twisting it with a satisfying crack that sends him to his knees. The bottle falls to the floor with a thud, the scent of spilled rum filling the air.

"I will not let you break her," I say.

"Who?" he screams, clutching his broken wrist.

"Ellen!"

"Ellen? The girl? She's mine, ya bastard," he spits. "I take good care of 'er!"

I grab his suspenders in both hands and haul him to his feet. "She's not yours to care for any longer. None of them are." With that, I sink my fangs into his neck.

He screams and flails, trying to pull away, but I'm locked onto his throat. His blood tastes disgusting, tainted with alcohol, but it fuels me.

With one hand, he pulls a small folding knife from his pocket and fumbles to open it. But once the blade appears, I slap it from his grip and it clatters to the floor.

He's losing strength, still trying to fight back, but his efforts weaken as his life's blood pours down my gullet.

Yes, I'll be leaving no doubt that a vampire caused his death, and they'll be looking for me. But in the worst case, I can just move on to another city. I've done it many times before.

But then I hear the door creak open behind me. I withdraw my fangs from Sutter's neck and pivot.

There she stands—Ellen—frozen in the doorway, eyes wide with horror. Why in Heaven's name did she return?

I release Sutter, his body collapsing to the floor, a whimper escaping his throat. My pupils, reduced to pinpricks by the ecstasy of feeding, and the blood trailing from my lips, surely create an image torn from Ellen's darkest nightmares.

She opens her mouth to scream.

"Be quiet," I command before the scream arrives. "Come inside and shut the door."

She nods, then shuts her mouth and quietly steps inside, closing the door behind her.

"You... you're a vampire," she says.

"Indeed I am. But I promise I won't hurt you, Ellen. Just him."

"Get help, woman," croaks Sutter, clutching a hand to his bleeding neck.

I look down at him and lock eyes with the man. "Sleep," I say.

He looks up at me in confusion, but then he shuts his eyes, goes slack, and starts snoring raggedly.

"Why are you doing this?" whispers Ellen, her voice trembling beneath the weight of her fear.

"For you," I say.

She looks down at the wretch at my feet. "I didn't ask you to hurt him."

"You didn't have to. This man was going to beat you, and for what? What crime have you committed against him?"

She shakes her head angrily. "I told you, he's my problem, not yours. Leave him be. He takes care of me."

"No," I say, stepping towards her. "He does not take care of you. He controls you. Allow me to free you from his torment."

"That's not your burden to bear, Drake. It's mine, and mine alone. It's for me to decide."

"For you to decide?" I turn back to the sleeping drunkard on the floor, then look back at her. "So *decide*. His fate rests in your hands now."

She recoils, taking a step backward—a movement I have seen before from her. It's a mirror of her retreat from Sutter's raised fist a few minutes earlier. I realize she fears me as she feared him then. In her eyes, I am not her savior but yet another image of cruelty.

"I can end Sutter's life this very moment," I declare. "He will hurt you no more. If you wish to continue this life, that is your choice, but there are men far less vile than him to oversee your efforts. He is nothing more than a monster—a parasite who feasts upon the weak."

"And you're not?" Her words strike deep, finding their mark within me.

"Perhaps I am," I say softly. "But if I'm a monster, then let me be the monster you need right now."

"I've done much that I regret," she mumbles. "But I've never caused a man's death."

"I've caused a few. What's one more?"

"I don't want his demise weighing upon my soul. I couldn't live with myself if I permitted someone to be killed, not even a wretched beast like him."

"You won't have to bear it," I reply. "I'll make you forget. Wipe your memory of everything that transpired in this room tonight. As easily as I made him sleep."

She looks down at his unconscious form, and I can see the tempest in her eyes. She loathes him, yes. She trembles at the thought of him. Does she dare allow herself the thought of being unshackled by his cruelty?

Her eyes rise to meet mine, a single tear carving a path down her cheek. "Alright, I've decided." She takes a deep, calming breath. "Kill the bastard."

I grin. "As you wish."

I pick up the discarded folding knife, its blade dull but sharp enough for my purposes. In one swift motion, I drag it across his throat. His life spills out onto the wooden floor in a crimson torrent.

He gurgles, spitting blood, but quickly goes still.

I stand, and she approaches me, her haunted eyes looking into mine. "Take it away. Make me forget."

"You will forget this happened," I command. "You saw nothing tonight. You were out and about when he died. When you hear of his death, it will be a shock to you. Understand?"

"I understand," she says in a monotone.

"Go now, and live."

She nods, her movements mechanical, and turns and leaves out the front door.

A week later, I stand at the banks of the Charles River, gazing out at the iron and steel expanse of the South Boston Bridge. I hold the morning newspaper in my hand, having read the article countless times already. It's about a woman named Ellen Leigh Reynolds.

I can't know for certain it's the woman I met that night. The first name is the only clear connection. But it's her nonetheless; I can feel it.

The hand-drawn image accompanying the story includes a solitary bird, black as night, perched upon the left shoulder of the faceless woman hanging by a rope from the bridge, its gaze fixed ahead, almost as if it were looking straight at me from within the newspaper.

She'd left a note, confessing an all-consuming guilt, but admitting she was unclear why she felt it.

Though I'd cast her memories into the void, guilt is not so easily undone, it seems. It leaves the deeper wound untouched. My mercy was no mercy whatsoever, but a torment all its own, cruel in its incomprehensibility.

Had she remembered her decision that chilly night, would the weight have been as heavy? Or might she have found some way to reconcile herself with it, to shoulder the burden and press on? By erasing her memory, it seems I had turned her guilt into an unfamiliar presence, one from which she could find no respite but by burning her life down altogether.

I turn and walk away from the bridge along the riverside, each step an attempt to put recent events further in my wake, to leave behind the unwanted specter of Ellen's memory.

I hear a caw and look up to see a dark bird, a raven, perched on the corner of a nearby building. It looks down at me and calls out again.

"Do you blame me, too?" I ask.

The bird tilts its head as if considering, then takes flight.

Dr. Lestrange
Editor/Graphic Artist

Marie Lestrange is a multipassionate badass that plays eight musical instruments and is deathly afraid of chickens. She's the author of gothic historical novels Crimson Cobblestones and The Devil's Colony. She hosts a weekly indie Horror podcast called Moths to the Flame. She's obsessed with research into the macabre, true crime, and occultish practices and is also the founding chairman of the Horror Writers Association Tennessee Chapter. When not writing, she and her writer husband, Bert, love traveling with their little Hobbit outside of the East Tennessee mountains they call home. https://linktr.ee/lestrangebooks

THE PHANTOM FLESH

Marie Lestrange

The Withering

Midnight's shroud envelops my cell,

As I gaze upon this unfamiliar shell.

Gone are the curves that once I adored,

Replaced by angles, sharp... abhorred?

My fingers trace bones, once hidden from sight,

Protruding now in pale moonlight.

Oft' I long for the softness of yore,

"Naturally" those lush curves return nevermore.

The Decay

Days pass, and still I wither away,

My form a flower in cruel decay.

Skin loosens, hanging like tattered lace,

A macabre mask upon a gaunt face.

Fear grips my heart as I continue to shrink,

My very essence threatens to sink.

Will I vanish, fade into the floor?

Quoth the spectre of my former

in the mirror, "Nevermore."

The Disgust

Weeks turn to months, and revulsion grows,

As my body's transformation shows.

Leathery flaps where curves once lay,

Melted wax, thinner frame on display.

Wrinkles deepen, mapping decline,

A topography of flesh malign.

I recoil from this sight I so deplore,

To love this form? Croaks my heart, "Nevermore."

The Excitement

But wait! A glimmer in these sunken eyes,

A thought both terrible and yet...p'haps wise?

With trembling hands, I grasp the shears,

To cut away these fleshy years.

Snip by snip, I shed the old,

Reveal a form both new and bold.

Excitement builds– skin falls to the floor,

To hate this body? I vow, "Nevermore!"

In an asylum of the mind and flesh,

I embrace my form, my look afresh.

Though changed by time and surgeon's knife,

I choose to claim an altered life.

Mirrors reflect a figure reborn,

No longer a subject of pity or scorn.

In moments of madness, I find my core,

And whisper to my reflection, "**Evermore.**"

Bert Lestrange

Bert Lestrange's works include various degrees of Horror, Fantasy, Weird Fiction, and, occasionally, unadulterated Smut. He is the husband of Marie Lestrange, a world traveler and a self-proclaimed foodie —though he has a weakness for gas station chili dogs. He and his family's roots spiderweb across the mountains of East Tennessee. Caregiver, father, and proud ally. Nicest asshole you'll ever meet. Find more of his writing on Godless.com, and two forthcoming novels, STOMPING GROUNDS and an untitled Vampire romance.

FOR WHOM THE PHONE BUZZES

BERT LESTRANGE

My phone buzzed again. I'd been ignoring it for the past two hours, but it was exactly eight minutes after midnight and I couldn't stand it any longer. She'd worn me down. Thirty-nine notifications, and each was the same.

> Hey

I suddenly realized the hour matched her date of birth. December the eighth.

> Blowing up my phone? Really? I seem to recall you screaming something about being done with my 'narcissistic bullshit'? Does that ring a bell?

The responses were immediate.

> I was wrong.

> I need you

Come back

Melissa is out of town. We'd have the whole room to ourselves. You should come over *winky face*. Maybe I can make it up to you? *smiley face*

Oh no, not falling for that again. Netflix and Chill devolves into hurt feelings and thrown objects. She collected acrylic dolphins, which were surprisingly heavy and sharp.

"I'm super horny rn. You can do that thing you like with my butt. *Eggplant* *Peach* *water* *winky face*."

Well... maybe I should hear her out. We did have more good memories than bad, even if the bad were, occasionally, somewhat violent...

I sighed, closing my laptop halfway through Cabin in the Woods. We'd watched that one more than a dozen times together. It usually ended early with her snoring in my lap or me pulling her hair while she screamed my name. It was a shame we usually missed the exquisite climax, but that was *my* sacrifice for the greater good.

She did this all the time. We fought and broke up; we kissed and made up. It was kind of our thing. After a while of messing around, or when I was close to dating someone else, she'd send one of these late-night booty call texts and like a horny fish, I was hooked all over again. We were basically The Notebook.

I grabbed my coat and pointed a stern finger into the nose of the man in the mirror.

One last dance and when it's over, you're done. End of statement.

It was a promise often made but never kept.

My phone buzzed just as I stepped into my car.

Lewd pictures manifested in a stacked line along with "Come and get it big boy!"

I did just under twenty over the limit—no need to be reckless—until rounding into her subdivision. As usual, I parked a street over and walked the rest. Her roommate never approved of us, so I climbed their back patio and slipped through the broken hinged window. Old habits die hard. They'd tried to fix it a dozen times, but the thing was old, crooked, and never stayed locked. A raven cawed in a nearby tree, which sent icy shivers down my spine for approximately three seconds. I couldn't locate the bird, but glancing inside stole its existence from my memory.

She was completely nude except for the wand buzzing furiously in her hand, and all of her delicacies were facing me.

"This is the last time. Okay? I'm not kidding anymore."

She moaned and bit her lower lip.

I dropped my trousers and boxers in a pile, followed by my socks. "I'm serious. You're so fucking toxic. We're bad for each other."

"Let me remind you just how good we can be, baby." She moaned.

I'm not a smart man, but I know not to turn down an offer like that. As my performance neared its apogee, I shuddered, rolling over beside her. I was lost in the sweet buzz of euphoria. She kissed me, but I was still too dazed to fight back. When my senses slowly returned, I decided to put my foot down.

"That was the last time, okay, Elenore? I'm serious. We can't just keep the fuck-fight cycle going."

She chuckled and gave a knowing wink. "But makeup sex is so hot! If you hang around, you might just get to enjoy your own sloppy seconds."

Swaying her hips as she went, she didn't bother putting on clothes before slipping out the door. She did stop long enough to give me that smile that meant the best was yet to come. The communal bathroom was down the hall. I hated using it because there were 11 other people in the house, and you never knew who'd come knocking.

"'My own sloppy seconds?.' Jesus, why do I keep falling for this?"

I snatched up my clothes and put them on. I needed to get away from this succubus before she lured me into her loins once again. I could already imagine the drop-down, drag-out that would follow. The fight was always directionally proportional to the fuck, and this had been a real banger. If it wasn't tomorrow, it'd be a week or two from now. Probably in an embarrassingly public location, like a crowded coffee shop or perhaps a bustling grocery store. She had a flair for the dramatic.

Just as I slipped on my shoes, I heard shuffling from behind the door.

Keys jingled and the lock clicked. But rather than Elenore, Susan "The Roommate" opened the door.

When she saw me, she dropped her keys and went pale.

"What the fuck are you doing here, Ed? You can't be here anymore. You know that."

I was thankful to be fully dressed this time.

"I know. I know. She just... I just can't stay away."

She paused, wringing her hands for a country minute before walking in and stopping a few feet from me. I could smell the beer on her breath. Another frat party, no doubt. So much for being out of town.

"You can't keep coming back here; you have to move on. You look like shit, and you need to leave."

I let out a long sigh and ran a hand through my sweat-soaked hair. It was nearly two in the morning.

"Thanks. That helps."

She shook her head.

"I'm sorry. I've been drinking. But this…" She motioned to me, then the window. "This can't keep happening. You need to find somewhere else. Someone else."

"I will. It just takes time, you know. After tonight, I'm done. Swear."

She actually put a hand on my shoulder, which was the closest thing to kindness she'd ever shown me. I almost asked her to give Elenore my farewells, but she interrupted my thoughts.

"Ed. I'm going to be real with you. Next time I catch you in my house, I'm calling the cops. Now, get the fuck out, ok? And use the front door like a normal human person. I'm replacing that window first thing tomorrow. And installing a security camera or something."

I walked to the door, thinking about waiting for her, My Raven, in the hallway. No… Nevermore. She could be someone else's problem from now on.

"Look, I know you're going through a lot. Everyone is, but I'm going to count down from ten. If I don't hear footsteps down the stairs, I'm calling 911. Got it?"

"Understood." I rolled my eyes and slammed the door on my way out.

I stomped on every step to make sure she heard me leaving.

It was an hour before my shift was over at The Boot Barn. I'd spent the last seven pretending to know everything about the damn things while not giving two shits about cowboy boots at all. But we earned bonuses for hitting sales goals, and twenty bucks is twenty bucks, before taxes, of course.

I have a problem. Wanna see if you can fin-ger it out? *wink* I need another taste.

My dick betrayed me, already stretching my trousers.

Steve was stoned out of his mind. He had a funny way of self-medicating to cope with the daily toil to avoid the fact that he had no real future.

"Steve. I'm about to gravy my pants. Think you can hold down the fort for ten minutes?"

He turned slowly, as if in a dream. His smile spread like February syrup.

"Sure, bro. I got this. Don't worry about pinching it off. No need to prairie-dog it. Go drop some logs, man." He paused, as though suddenly realizing something. "And... I dunno how to say it. Words aren't really my thing. I can hook you up or smoke you out or something. Just let me know, bro."

I nodded gratefully. "Thanks, dude. I owe you one."

He was oddly concerned with my gastric health, but I appreciated the offer. Half jogging to sell the lie, I threw open the restroom door and found a stall before returning to my phone.

> You know we can't. That was the last time, remember?

> Not if I have anything to say about it, babe. Tell me all about it with my head in your lap.

> No. Seriously, I'm done with you. It's not healthy.

> But I'm not done with you. Not yet. It's basically exercise. Exercise is healthy right?

> Why are you like this?

> You are my drug. I'm addicted. It's almost Thanksgiving. Come stuff this turkey.

That was an inside joke and brought back filthy memories. The pictures that followed sold me on the idea.

> Ok. You can suck me off, but I'm not getting anywhere near your treachery hole. Understood?

Mmmmmmm! Yes sir! Come fuck my mouth and we'll just see what happens. I'll be waiting for you behind the movie theater.

We almost got caught there last time. Let's go somewhere else?

She sent a picture of her clothes piled up on her car with the rear of the movies in the background.

Better hurry before somebody decides to take your place. Does Zach still work here? He's pretty cute.

I tugged a few hairs from my scraggly beard. Why did I let her do this?

Just hold on, you whore. I'll be there as soon as I can.

You've got fifteen minutes before I go hunting for some strange.

I almost told her to just do it. Maybe that would help me cope, but my lower head got the better of me.

Let me see if Steve can cover

Steve was more than happy to finish the shift alone. It only cost me twenty bucks, untaxed, of course.

The next day I regretted my decisions, but couldn't deny the mistake was fun. We hadn't been caught, but it was a very near thing. An officer pulled around shortly after she left and followed me all the way home.

It was my day off and I had intentions of watching football, eating wings, and drinking pitchers of beer until I didn't care how bad my team was.

WYD?

Not you.

I considered my phone's flood of buzzing before tossing it on the couch. Not today. I left it downstairs while showering. It started nice and hot, but I remained until it was cold enough to sober me. Post-nut clarity sometimes requires assistance.

Refreshed and refocused, I returned to thirty similar messages. The last was:

What are you doing today? I want to talk about something important. No sex, no games, just talk.

Shit. Was she pregnant? My stomach dropped into some abyss. We'd had a few scares over the years, but she was begrudgingly willing to take care of it as long as I paid the costs. Dreams of chicken and alcohol, surrounded by half-dressed waitresses, flew right out the window.

Fuck. That was an ill omen if there ever was one.

Our spot was about a mile hike into the woods. There were trails, but at a certain dead tree, one could take a left turn off the trail and quickly find oneself on a bluff beside a small mountain river. In the spring, mountain laurels bloomed into a romantic scene that was straight out of a Nicholas Sparks novel. There was even a log that served as a perfect seat and plenty of soft grass for picnic blankets. We'd roasted marshmallows and read books together in the spot. It was our go-to for cheap dates.

I took my time arriving and had to sit in the car for half an hour before the cop riding my ass left the scene. It seemed the local police department was in dire need of funding. They seemed to be everywhere I went since my encounter with "The Roommate." She must have said something. She was a bitch, but I understood the logic.

Hoping to soften the blow, I stopped for sandwich fixings and carried the grocery bag opposite our picnic blanket.

It was an easy trail, and the hike eased my anxiety. It would be just like the other times. We'd sit down and have "the talk" before she agreed to an abortion, but only under the condition that we got back together. It was blackmail, but better than eighteen years of emotional and financial responsibility—post-tax, of course.

In the fall, for about two weeks, the trees were uniquely beautiful. It was an effervescent painting of exquisite color: rich browns, vibrant yellows, and brilliant crimson leaves. But that time had passed. The leaves were crunchy, and the landscape was dead, devoid of life beyond the occasional scampering squirrel.

My phone buzzed consistently, but I tried to ignore it. I was already here, dammit. We could talk when I arrived.

At the oak, my anxiety exploded out of nowhere. Heart racing, I had to brace myself against the tree. But why? I'd already rationalized the outcome. Even if it meant staying with her a few more weeks, what of it?

But this time was different; something was wrong. Bad wrong. Why did I feel so guilty? Surely the other times hadn't been this way? Steeling my resolve, I took the plunge. Five minutes later I found myself at what had been "our spot." She hadn't arrived yet, so I sat on the log. I started making a sandwich knowing it would be wasted by the absence of appetite. Neither of us would be hungry.

The phone in my pocket continued to buzz periodically.

The scene was cold and lifeless, only the river below made a sound. For some reason it smelled horrible, like rotten meat or something. Coyotes probably claimed a meal nearby, or maybe wolves. I stared into nothingness, dissociating as I was prone to do, trying to ignore the odor. Somewhere along the line, my eyes focused on a rock; it had a rusty crimson patina on one side, but the other was jagged and grey.

I picked it up with mild interest and was struck with the most curious sense of déjà vu. It felt good in my hand, not much larger than a softball with plenty of heft. I probably could have thrown it across the river, but not much farther.

When my phone buzzed again, in a moment of rage, I pulled it out and flung it as hard as I could. It skipped twice before plooping beneath the choppy waters. I'd regret that later, but right now I was so done with it. The thing had been driving me insane.

My attention returned to the stone, and I turned it over and over. The red color was so reminiscent of dried blood.

The phone buzzed again, and I reached for it before remembering I'd chucked it. I realized the sound hadn't come from my pocket. It was behind me. Dread filled every inch of my being as I turned. The vibration was incessant, less than two to five seconds between each new ring. It couldn't be mine, so what the fuck was it?

I shoved aside the bushes and was met with a sight that chilled my soul. Her body was rotting, desiccated and ruined. Something had eaten away at her eyes so that now only empty sockets stared up at me with betrayal. Her lips were gone, and both the wicked grin and crater in her skull dripped with a writhing mass of maggots.

Stumbling backward, I nearly fell into the river. As I landed flat on my ass, the memories resurfaced. The last time we'd been here had only been two weeks ago.

She was pregnant and intended to keep it. Nearly a dozen positive tests were presented as evidence. I offered to pay for another abortion and she vehemently refused. Past guilt was consuming her, and she wanted to make it right this time. I begged and bartered, but she shook her head and rubbed her belly. This would be the thing that brought us together, once and for all. This would be our glue.

Turning my head, I saw the rock which had been completely grey to begin that day. Some horrible, deep-seated fear had taken over, some primal need to protect myself from fatherhood. She hadn't seen the first blow coming, but she stared with wide eyes at the second and third. I don't think she was conscious for the rest, but her eyes never stopped staring. I remembered everything.

I ran from it. From her, from our spot, and from the heinous thing I'd done. The buzzing phone in my pocket was a phantom, but it refused to stop. It was her ghost punishing me. The telltale sign of guilt. My brain raced around the past week. The curious things her roommate had said. Steve's weird response.

Had I been hallucinating her this whole time?

As I burst through the trailhead, I found myself surrounded by half a dozen police cruisers with light bars whirling. One of them was a K-9 unit, and three dogs were sniffing around my car. A distant part of my brain asked me if they needed a warrant for that, but the question never formed on my lips as a rough hand crushed my collarbone. Two more were dragging their handlers back along the trail.

"Hello, Ed. We have a few questions about your ex-girlfriend Raven. It seems she hasn't been home in a couple of weeks, but you've been there several times. That's a bit strange, don't you think? You're going to need to come with us to the station for questioning."

He looked down at the stone in my hand and tilted his head while raising an eyebrow. "Souvenir? You're not supposed to take things from the forest... Jesus, is that blood?"

I dissociated completely and found myself handcuffed in the back of a cruiser some undetermined time later. My pocket buzzed incessantly. Then, just as quickly, I was in a room with white walls except for a single mirrored window and door. I wore an orange suit with numbers across it. My hands were cuffed to the chair behind me, and Polaroids depicting Elanore's corpse and the pages of our phone records were spread across the steel table in front of me while an officer stared pure hatred into my soul.

"I swear to God, it's like you have split personalities. First you cry, then you go stoic, and now you look drunk. You seem present now, at least. So, let's try this one more time... You went to her house, knowing she wasn't there, returned to the scene of the murder, and destroyed your phone. You have to know how this looks. Hell, you handed the murder weapon to Bob yourself. It won't help you in court, but it might clear your conscience if you just admitted to killing Elenore. It would make our jobs easier and the record could be clean; tucked away neat and tidy and sealed with a bow. Talk to me, Ed. We have all day together."

The pants I wore didn't even have pockets, but the phantom phone against my thigh just buzzed and buzzed and buzzed.

Carietta Dorsch

Carietta Dorsch has loved horror movies since she was a little girl watching them at a way too earlier age and loves even more to share her love of horror with her writing. She also writes poetry, romance, and true crime. Find more of her work "O Come All Ye Fearful," "Never Be Lonely Again," "Scream and Cream," "The Mitchell County Stories," "Cannibalistic Loneliness," and "Tattered."

RAVEN

Carietta Dorsch

Whispers of true love haunt me in the dead of the night,
Echoes of laughter and much-needed tender delight.
My memories linger with bittersweet pain,
In the depths of my soul, she will forever remain.

I am destined for loneliness; I shall walk alone,
A ghost of my past, a heart turned to stone.
This emptiness inside, this void so deep,
Calls out with echoes of promises I know I can't keep.

I can hear the raven call out my name

In the shadows, her presence is still there,
In my dreams, her touch still lingers so fair.
A love once cherished, is now lost in time,
Fading away just like a distant chime.

I wander in solitude, lost in my self-hate,
Seeking solace in memories that can no longer wait.
Burdened by the weight of what could have been,
A love so pure, now tainted by sin.

I can hear the raven call out my name

Haunted by the ghost of a love now lost,
I shall carry the burden, no matter the cost.
In the silence of my heart's endless plea,
I know true love will never set me free.

Destined for loneliness, my path unclear,
In the echoes of my past, she still appears.
Yet in the darkness of my mind, a glimmer of light,
A hope that one day, my heart may take flight.

I can hear the raven call out my name

For love's eternal flame can never truly die,
In the depths of my soul, it will always lie.
Though destined for loneliness, I'll find my way,
Towards a brighter tomorrow, and a brand new day.

Then I saw her
Oh, I saw her
I heard the raven yet again call out my name
Whispering its warnings and retelling my shame

Nevermore raven, I will not listen to you
What you say, or what you tell me to do
She is too beautiful to not talk to
And I am oh so lonely

Go away raven, I say
Yet its cry doesn't leave, and its call rings out for all to hear and
all to say
Raven, please leave me and just go away

It finally takes flight as I take her in
Eyes scanning her beauty

I first saw her, her eyes so green
shocked by her beauty, so luscious and clean
In the realm of thoughts, did beauty appear,
A woman ethereal, drawing ever so near.
With each passing glance, a spark ignited bright,

Her beauty captivating, a mesmerizing light.

In the garden of the mind, she wandered free,
Her presence growing, a symphony.
Her radiance eclipsing all in my sight,
A vision of beauty, stunning in all its might.

As days turned into nights, she lingered in me still,
Her image haunting, a persistent thrill.
In every word, in every fleeting gesture,
Her beauty held captive, a treasure to treasure.

With each passing moment, she grew in power,
In my mind's eye, a blooming flower.
Thoughts consumed by my allure,
A beauty unmatched, she'd forever be pure.

And as she danced within my mind's embrace,
Her beauty etched, a portrait's grace.
An obsession bloomed, a love so rare,
Her beauty consuming, beyond compare.

Entwined in her beauty, mind and soul,
A vision extraordinary, a captivating stroll.

In the depths of fascination, she did dwell,
Her beauty's essence, a magical spell.

And in this tale of beauty's endless hold,
A philosophical truth begins to unfold.
For in the watching of beauty divine,
We glimpse a truth that forever will shine.

A reflection of the soul, an inner light,
Beauty's allure, a beacon so bright.
In watching the most beautiful woman, I may find,
A connection to the sublime, to the heart and mind.

The raven cries out a warning
But for me or for her
I can not tell, but the warning is heard
She sees me watching and runs away

I will make her mine
for she will accept my offer or she will die
With every smile, a spell was cast,
Obsession bloomed, the die was cast.
Her laughter echoed in my restless mind,
As obsession took root, was not far behind.

I followed her shadow, a hopeless chase,
Obsession burning bright in love's embrace.
Every thought consumed, every breath a sigh,
As passion turned to obsession under moonlit sky.

I watched her like a hawk, her every move I knew,
Obsession grew and obsession grew, my entire world now askew.
A prisoner of love, trapped in my own desire,
burning like a restless fire.

But love turned dark, twisted by my need,
Obsession's grasp now choked the seed.
A once pure love, now tainted and flawed,
Obsession's descent, a path untrod.

I put the knife up against her throat
knowing she would let out that final note
her breath a gasp and then a sigh
as I watched death flee from her green eyes
she grasped my chest and contdinued to bleed
as my obsession gave forth its final deed

I loved her, I did, just like the last

but I can no longer love, for that's in my past
each love I have a body does fall
for love is obsession and obsession consumes my all

The raven calls out my name in the dead of the night
Hoping to warn them, so that they can all take flight
But no matter—I will find, I will search every night
For the last breath on my hands is such a delight.

L.W. Young

L.W. Young graduated from the University of Kent with a BA Honors degree in English literature and creative writing. He has experience with writing for theater, film and YouTube, and is a passionate advocate of mindfulness and raising awareness of mental health issues. His favourite authors and influences include an eclectic bag: ranging from Stephen King to Cormac McCarthy to Ray chandler to David Mitchell to Kazuyo Ishigoda to Margaret Atwood and Colson Whitehead. However, if you ask him, he would probably tell you his favourite books are the Point Horror novels he read in his High School library as a teenager. His haunting novella, THE OCCUPANT, debuts April 2025.

DEATH WINGS

L.W. Young

Night was descending.

Blowing sweaty, tangled hair away from her eyes, May snatched the nozzle and twisted it with both arms. She needed boiling water to defend herself from those things when she went back outside. With tears building in her eyes, she remembered the long-ago fresh winter mornings when she would use this water to defrost the birdbath.

It felt like another life now. As she drew water into the bucket, the basement bulb popped, making her shriek. In the darkness, sweat rolled off her face. Throaty, screeching caws from outside were all she could hear, mocking her. Perhaps they had sabotaged the generator, too.

"Shut up," she grunted through clenched teeth as the noises circled her, barely softened by the basement walls. "Shut up!"

But it was no use. She knew they wouldn't stop until she was dead. After all, such birds only fed on decaying matter.

A year ago, it had all been so different. May had come to this secluded cabin with little but the clothes on her back to get away from the city. A log fire, forest pine air, thatched roof, and foraged meals were all she thought she had needed. What nature offered was so much cleaner, so much purer than the suffocation of the city. The smoke. The noise. The drama. May hadn't been able to stand it any longer.

Without saying a word to her remaining friends and family about where she was going, May had carved out a new life for herself in these secluded hills, with little company but the birds that visited her each morning. May didn't mind, as she felt the birds understood her more than people did.

And that was how it had stayed for the longest time, just her and the birds.

It hadn't been perfect, however. The longer May remained in the wilderness, the more she became afflicted by bouts of hunger and anxiety.

"They're meaningless sensations, caused only by my lingering attachment to the old world," May had told herself on one cold and windy night while rocking on her bed with her blanket pulled tightly around her. "Let them go."

She had tried, and it had eventually worked, although she still sometimes found herself surprised by the sound of her own voice and, one day, had even jumped at the sight of her own reflection in one of her steel cooking pans.

However, none of this truly mattered when she had the birds for company. The more time she'd committed to cultivating the little community in the front yard, the more she'd been rewarded by their colour, beauty, and music. There were regular guests like the common robins and song thrushes, and then there were the sometimes visitors like jays, sparrows, and even woodpeckers.

After a few weeks, May had decided that the hunger and loneliness was worth it. For the first time that she could remember, there were no problems in her life.

But then they started to arrive.

From day one, May had sensed their evil scent before she'd even laid eyes on them. One morning, she'd simply been woken up by it: the lingering smell of death just outside her front door. She'd opened the door to instantly be attacked by a schism of long black wings and sharp beaks, many of them fighting to get inside her sanctuary.

With cuts and claw marks all over her, May had managed to shut them out of her cabin as they kept banging and scraping against the door. May hadn't thought it had been possible for her to hate a bird as much as a person, but her feelings were confirmed for them straight away.

At first, May had wondered if, with the help of some tactically placed poison feed, she could deal with the black horrors if they stayed at their current numbers. But each day, more and more came to land, scaring away her usual friends. And they stank like rotting meat, unnaturally waking her from restless dreams every morning.

She couldn't find them in any textbook: tar-black feathers, far larger than crows, ruby-red beaks, and glowing orange eyes. They travelled in packs and made a relentless scraping call. And they were always hungry. Once, she ran out to shoo them off, but they had remained in place, their glowing eyes staring back at her. Caw. Caw.

Their beaks could tear through feeders, even expensive ones. And her regular visitors? These horrid birds hadn't been so keen on *them*. May still remembered emerging from a bad night's sleep to shake out food for her little buddies, only to see a bloody heap of them piled up beneath a departing curtain of flapping black wings.

At this point, May had been left with no choice but to call upon the services of the old world for help. Pest control. Of course, it had taken them a while to find May's secluded little cabin, and when the two slack-jawed idiots *did* arrive to inspect, the winged demons had chosen to be nowhere in sight.

"Sounds to me like they might be Corvids," the first inspector had said while scratching his backside. "Red-beaked birds that feed on decaying matter and carry disease? Might explain the dead ones."

"But it's not the disease that's killing my... my friends," May had tried to explain, "*they're* killing them!"

"Sometimes seagulls come out into the mainland," the other inspector had inserted, "they can be quite aggressive..."

"But they're not seagulls!" May had almost screamed at them both. "So what *are* they?"

The inspectors had left without being able to answer, and when it became clear that she could offer them little money in exchange for their services, had not shown much interest in helping further. With their lack of answers, May had invented a new name for the awful creatures: Death Wings. It seemed fitting.

From that day, May made it her mission to rid herself of the Death Wings, putting every other survival priority on hold until she succeeded. No more sleeping. No more washing. No more eating. This cabin, this corner of the world she'd carved out for herself, was the only thing in her entire life that was truly hers, and she was not about to let the Death Wings take it.

She would do whatever it took.

Now, she was stamping up the cellar stairs, barely noticing the sloshing water that scalded her hands.

"I'll have done with you," she panted as she hauled the steaming metal bucket through the darkened house towards the front door. "I'll have done with you ALL!"

Outside the cabin, shifting patterns of red and black smothered the gaps in the log-built walls, and beaks tapped relentlessly on the wood. Tap. Tap. Tap. Of course, the cawing remained, but it had now grown to a fever pitch of white noise matched only by the raging fury in her head. Charging at her front door, May stumbled out with the burning bucket at the ready, but a black whirlwind erupted around her, making her drop it. She threw her hands to her face.

And in the twilight sky, she peered through her fingers to see that the descending dark cloud was not the coming of nightfall, but something far worse...

THE END

Rian Burnhouse

Rian Burnhouse is a lifelong fan of fantasy novels, which has translated into a love for writing his own fantasy works and creating Dungeons & Dragons content for his quickly growing YouTube channel. He is currently writing his first novel while growing his fan base as "Dad the Dungeon Master" on YouTube. He spends his free time enjoying his family, writing short stories, and running tabletop games for his friends and YT followers.

THE DAEMON

RIAN BURNHOUSE

On midnight winds ever drifting,
while I sailed on drafts uplifting
Over sands so softly shifting,
along the broken, craggy shore
Here I found my proper landing,
barely room for one bird standing
Rapping curtly, beak demanding,
Man within I do implore
Open up and swiftly grant me,
Respite from this chill downpour
To complete my gruesome chore

A gift I bring on darkened nights,
A master called, a bird's swift flight
In others' pain I must delight,
This is what I was made for

The man inside, near to sleeping,
In his anguish he was steeping,
A silent wish, quiet reaping,
Men like him I'd helped before
To take their hurt with mythic magic,
A silent wraith from ancient lore
This my task, forevermore

As I tapped the tattered shutter
Within he began to mutter
His mind, it seemed, filled with clutter
Like other men I'd seen before
As he sat there surely seeming,
Like a man awake, but dreaming
I knew I would be relieving
Pain for which there was no cure
I rapped again, tapping faster,
But his head turned towards the door
Speaking louder than before

Then he stood and started shouting,
Words of pain and pious pouting
Such anguish that I stood doubting
Sadder words were said before

Upon his face he did emboss,
Contorted cracks of pain and loss,
As he moved, did his shadow cross,
To rest upon his ornate door
Here he gathered up his courage,
Flinging open wide the door
He is lost of that, I'm sure

There he stood, in darkness staring,
With his discontented bearing
Looking at the darkness glaring,
Softly he spoke, one word, "Lenore?"
This I knew was his lost lover,
From her loss he'll ne'er recover
Respite from pain, he'll discover,
I'll soon make him forget Lenore
I the winged wish unspoken,
Called to a hurt I can't ignore
That's what I was sent here for

When he spun, his grief returning,
Summoned I, my strength and yearning
And resumed my fervent rapping,
Somewhat harder than before

There again he started squawking,
This sad soul obsessed with talking
Across the room he came walking,
Finally he won't ignore
I prepared to make my entrance,
None like me, he's seen before
I'll change his life evermore

Open now he swung the shutter, I,
With a brilliant flirt and flutter
Stepped inside with regal bearing,
To form a fairly firm rapport
No time now for hollow greeting,
Up I swept to find my seating
A fine place to start entreating,
I found above his chamber door
I'd say the sight of such a shadow,
He has never seen before
Sorrow brought me, nothing more

Then the broken man was smiling,
To himself he was beguiling
Not aware of my reviling,
Or the cause I was here for

Here he tried a slick embellish,
Hoping that his words I'd relish,
My private past, more than hellish,
He said "Your name? I do implore!"
Ancient oaths my soul had spoken,
My name I lost forevermore
My curt response: "Nevermore"

Thus he stood confused and staring,
Unaware of my dark daring,
Deep within me pity flaring,
For broken men with shattered core
No man or beast could e'er resist
When my dark master does insist
The reason that I do exist,
Is to destroy what came before
So I channeled ancient magic,
That came from deep within my core
To be repaired Nevermore

While he stood there calmly musing,
My malediction perfusing
Dark magic his soul infusing,
To cleanse his mind of lost Lenore

But he gripped her grace so tightly,
In his soul her face burned brightly
Resisting my hex so knightly,
Sterner than I'd seen before
Neither did my spell affect him,
Nor would he let go Lenore
This was harder than before

What silly sad situation,
Stuck inside his self made station,
Fighting from my faux ablation,
That would free him from Lenore,
Unaware his fate, I authored,
Question after question proffered
One response was all I offered,
The same response he got before,
No matter how I wished to answer,
My master wouldn't grant me more
My one recourse "Nevermore"

Now, before me, his seat he moved,
This smiling fool, resilience proved
Sullen memories won't be removed
Deeper I pressed, more than before

Still this harrowed and heartbroken,
Man whose interest had awoken
Still resisted my dark token,
To take the pain of lost Lenore
His psyche fought without his knowledge,
Clinging sternly to Lenore
Must I push more than before?

Hard I pressed my hex impressing,
Deep within him, doubts repressing,
Still his stubborn thoughts caressing,
Faded memories of Lenore
What will it take to tame his heated,
Fancies that he's long repeated,
My best attempts he has defeated,
To rend his thoughts, remove Lenore
I've pressed as much as I have ever,
No mind ever held before
I suppose I must take more

Finally he sensed my passion,
His facade failed him, falling ashen
His soul perhaps, could refashion
Here he shouted, asking more

Screaming, pleading, wanting mercy,
Dreaming I could play his Circe
But inside him controversy,
He could not let go Lenore
In order to grant his wishes,
Out my master I must pour
So I warned him, "Nevermore"

Now he sensed my mystic nature,
Asking for a saintly tincture,
He begged some holy prelature
That could offer him a cure
Hark I thought, but I tried that path
Respite for him I did not hath,
Beyond my master's mythic wrath
That would take more than Lenore
My master's wholly, full, undaunted,
Power breaks men to their core
Again I warned, "Nevermore"

As I poured out ancient power,
Mind and heart meant to devour
One last question, cold and dour
Had I ever seen Lenore

This request I deemed to honor,
Distant realms my thoughts upon her,
Master's curse, I can't dishonor
It won't allow me to say more
The first and last time I regret,
For what my master sent me for
I spoke falsehood, "Nevermore"

At this, he broke, started shouting,
Like a child's raucous pouting
Turned on me, attempted routing
Cursing me from off his door
But my work was almost finished
His hold on hope had diminished
Reality would soon be finished
My dark task I now abhor
To break his mind and melt his soul,
He'd be a husk, nothing more
I wailed protest, "Nevermore"

With empty heart, my task was done
My master's mythic magic won
His mind is shattered, heart undone
He drops his gaze down to the floor

And with his gaze, my soul has dropped

I wish my master I had stopped,

With every task my soul is chopped

Its pieces scattered on the floor

His soul and mine both shattered remnants,

That lie scattered on the floor

Shall be lifted-Nevermore

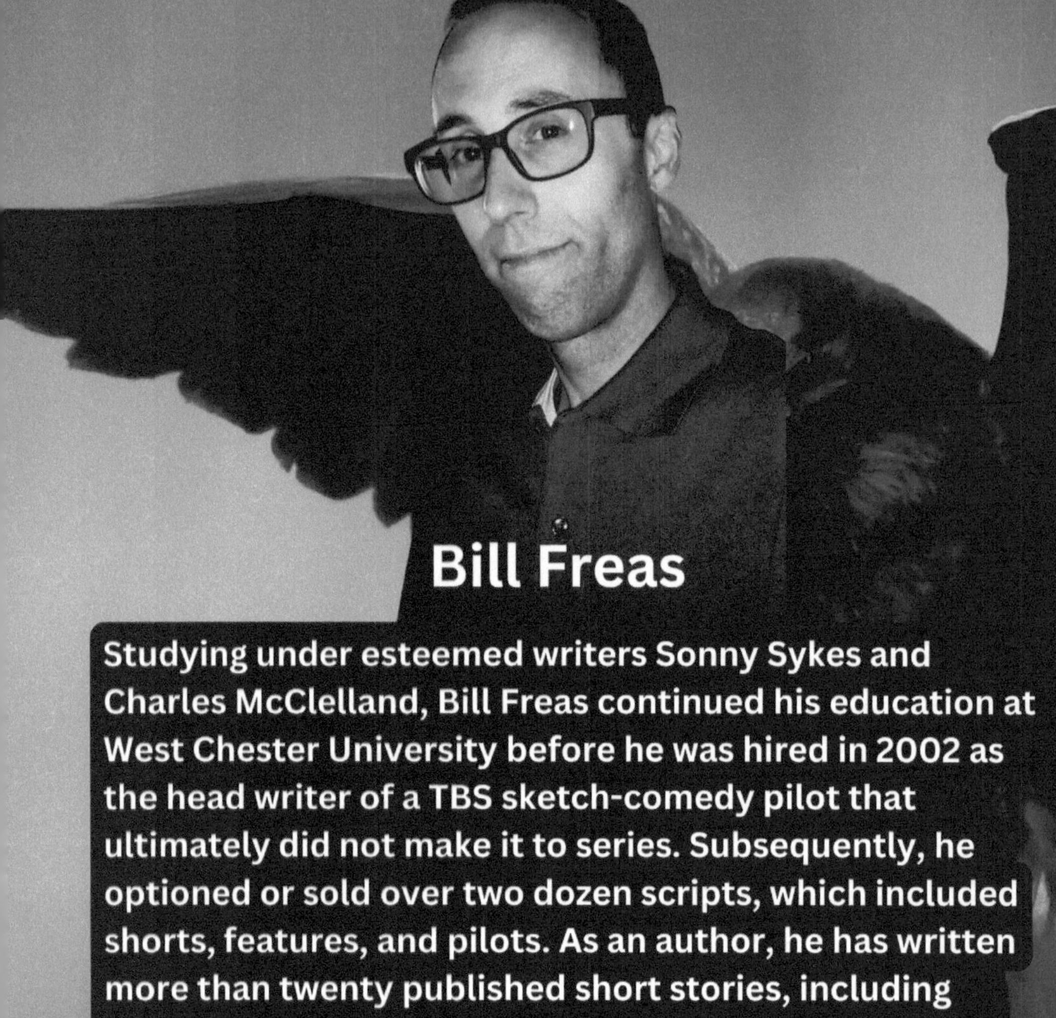

Bill Freas

Studying under esteemed writers Sonny Sykes and Charles McClelland, Bill Freas continued his education at West Chester University before he was hired in 2002 as the head writer of a TBS sketch-comedy pilot that ultimately did not make it to series. Subsequently, he optioned or sold over two dozen scripts, which included shorts, features, and pilots. As an author, he has written more than twenty published short stories, including three full collections. His produced credits as a writer span multiple genres and mediums. Currently, Bill also heads up Oceanicom Films' development department, where he oversees the development of US and international film and TV projects for the Australian company. Along with script, development, and production consultation, Bill is also a staff writer for Vancouver production company Foresight Entertainment, with which he has had an active partnership for over fifteen years.

4TH AND DEAD

BILL FREAS

T hunder rumbled off in the distance as the cold rain came down harder on M&T Stadium in downtown Baltimore. It was late in the third quarter, fourth and goal at the five-yard line, and Ravens quarterback Frankie Macomb needed a touchdown to get his team back in this game, which was getting out of reach for them.

In fact, the whole season was falling out of reach for the team, particularly the all-star QB, whose play had spiraled downward ever since the tragic and somewhat mysterious death of his wife six months earlier.

Long slugs of rain slapped his helmet and drowned out the sound of the desperate crowd. He took the snap from his center, his hands barely able to grip the slick pigskin. He stepped back into a five-step drop as the opposition's defense sent six rushers at him. Frankie acted fast and rolled out to his right, nearly slipping on the wet turf.

He looked through the sheets of thickening precipitation for an open receiver. Finally, his eyes locked in on Thorman, the starting tight end, who was separating from the tight coverage of a fast and tenacious linebacker and was running right behind and parallel to the goal line. As the pass rush got too close for comfort, Frankie threw a rocket, but it was too far in front of his surging tight end. Instead, the throw was picked off by an opportunistic cornerback lurking in that area of the end zone.

The crowd let out a massive groan of disappointment as the cornerback raced in the other direction for a pick-six. Frankie stood there with his head lowered. When he found the courage to look up again, he saw an arena full of angry faces shouting at him. This was a mere microcosm of his life for the last six months. As he trudged back to the sideline, his defeated eyes met Poe, the Ravens mascot, who stood off to the side, about a hundred feet away, staring at him, motionless.

The game couldn't have ended fast enough. It eventually did, with the Ravens losing 31-12 and dropping to 3-7 on their dismal, fading season. Heading into the locker room, Frankie steered clear of his teammates, knowing that they were as frustrated with him as he was with himself. Sadly, he just couldn't connect his mind and body productively anymore.

He avoided the press, too. There were too many awkward questions to answer and deep, dark things to address. His brain was pulsing with anxiety these days, and he needed his space. That space, in physical form, was an unused office far away on the other end of the tunnel corridor.

He tucked himself away in the dingy room, huddling up in the corner. A dim overhead light provided a depressing glow that only pushed him lower into his morose state. After ten minutes of serious contemplation and mental rambling, he took a folded piece of paper from out of his pocket. Opening it up, he read the scratchy writing for the umpteenth time today.

Lenore is no more. You cannot deny. I'm watching you closely. Soon, you'll be mine.

A loud rap on the door startled the man, nearly sending him through the roof.

He hesitated. "Who's there?"

There wasn't an immediate answer, just another booming knock.

"Who the hell is there?"

After a pause, a familiar male voice answered on the other side of the door. "The only person you told about hiding out in this room, Frankie. Now, open the goddamn door, please."

Frankie reached over and immediately unlocked the door. Walt Hazelman, quarterback coach and true father figure to Frankie, entered the room, gently closing the door behind him.

"Y'know, kid… at some point, they're gonna need to give this office to some dumbass intern or moron, entry-level quality-control coach. Where will you hide then?"

Frankie grimaced. "I won't have to worry about that too much longer. I imagine Jeff and Lou will cut me before the San Diego game."

Walt stepped closer and knelt down to console his football son. "Look… everybody has bad games. The best of the best even have bad seasons. This is one of 'em for you. You're the glue of this squad. You made the all-star team last year, for Christ's sake. You'll bounce back."

Frankie gazed down hopelessly.

"I know this has been… a tough year for you, pal," said Walt. "There's no denying that. You were dealt a real shit hand. But you gotta get up and move on… for Lenore. She'd want it that way, and you know that. She'd kick your sorry ass right now if she saw you sitting here sulking like a sad pile of shit in this dump of an office."

Frankie handed his coach the piece of paper. Walt looked it over and did an admirable job in not showing any visible concern over the unsettling words.

"Eh, another nut job. What's new?" he said.

"It's the third one this month. Same handwriting and always a poem," Frankie said. "It creeps me out when they mention Lenore in these things."

"I don't know what you want me to say, kid. The world's filled with crazy assholes, and none of 'em are on your side when you're losing football games."

"So, this is all just going to go away if we start winning again?" Frankie inquired.

Walt groaned and sighed with aches and pains as he stood up. "Maybe. Maybe not. Fame is a funny thing, pal. Sometimes, it's your best friend. Sometimes, your worst enemy. But it's always good at keeping you on your toes." He strolled over to the door. "Don't take all the bullshit too seriously, kid. This too shall pass, as they say. And don't hang out in here too long, either. This place is depressing. See you tomorrow for meetings. 10 AM."

Walt left the office and closed the door behind him. Frankie sat for a moment and took in his words, trying to make sense of it all.

Surprisingly, there was another hard, aggressive knock at the door, just like before.

"Yeah..." Frankie called out. There was no answer. "Did you forget your keys, Walt, or did you just want to bust my balls a little longer?"

Again, he received no reply. Instead, there were five knocks on the door, even harder and more forceful than the first one. Frankie held still and watched the door silently. Something felt off here.

"Walt? That you?"

Once again, there was no answer. This time, however, there was also no more knocking. An eerie hush permeated the atmosphere, as if a dark presence was close.

Frankie rose to his feet and stepped softly to the door. After taking a moment to gather his courage, he whipped open the door and peeked out into the tunnel hallway. There was no one around anywhere to be seen, and the long, empty hall was completely still and quiet.

Frankie's eyes were soon drawn to the floor, where a long, black feather seemed deliberately placed right in front of the door to the office. He reached down and picked it up to investigate. It was the feather of a raven, spattered with a few drops of blood. This was not the first time one of these was strategically positioned for him to find.

Frankie marched swiftly down the hallway. He had enough that night and was ready to sneak out and head home to drown his sorrows in some vodka and painkillers, both of which he was growing increasingly dependent on.

A small elevator took him from the hallway and down into the underground parking garage for players and executive staff. Like the isolated office he used as a hiding spot, the parking quarters were empty and quiet. It appeared that mostly everyone had left. Frankie couldn't even be sure how much time had passed between the end of the game and this point right now. The night was becoming a blur.

He felt his clothes for his cell phone, but it wasn't there—probably still in his locker upstairs. He forged on anyway, trekking to his BMW, which was parked all alone in a row that was back against a concrete wall on the far side.

Gripping his key fob tightly, he just couldn't shake that foreboding feeling he acquired in his hiding spot a little while ago. When he got closer to his car, he pressed the unlock button on the key fob but noticed that the vehicle was already unlocked. To his dread, he also observed that all four tires were slashed, the doors were keyed, and his windshield was cracked.

"What the fuck..." he muttered to himself.

He stepped over to the windshield and found another black feather, this one tucked under the bent driver-side wiper blade, accompanied by another note. The worried man peered around before removing the note and reading its familiar scratchy handwriting:

Nowhere to run, nowhere to hide. Just like Lenore, soon you will die.

Frankie's worry turned to rage. He moved away from his damaged vehicle and out into the open thoroughfare.

"What do you want from me?! Huh?! What is it?! Come out here, show yourself, you fucking psycho!"

With fire burning in his belly, he spun around and saw Poe, the Ravens mascot, standing motionless and staring at him about fifty feet away, just like that odd moment during the game.

"You... Did *you* do this? Huh?... Answer me! What's your problem?!" Frankie asked.

The mascot gave no reply, only the same ominous stare. Suddenly, the quick taps of running footsteps echoed behind Frankie, drawing closer with each stride. The quarterback spun around to face the other direction and observed an incoming attacker.

It was a man dressed in a black jumpsuit and a frightening, homemade raven mask. His violent determination was visible in his movements, and he held an axe with two strangely curved blades and a long, pointy spike separating them—a medieval battle instrument. The shiny steel of the intimidating weapon gleamed as it passed under the subtle overhead lighting fixtures in the garage.

"Hey! Hey, stop, man! Yo!" Frankie shouted. "Help! Help me!"

The attacker continued to pursue, raising his axe and preparing to strike. Frankie backed up and lifted his arm in a defensive position, just as the attacker swung the axe. One of the sharp blades sliced the quarterback's throwing arm, gashing it open with a six-inch laceration. Frankie let out a painful yelp and ran off, leaving a trail of blood.

The attacker rebalanced and continued the chase. Frankie dashed by Poe, who remained standing and watching in a strange and eerie manner. The oddly mesmerizing distraction caused Frankie to trip on the edge of a parking curb, sending him down hard to the ground, where he bumped his head. Poe continued staring but soon opened his wings slowly like a foreboding harbinger of death.

Dazed, Frankie rolled over and gathered his bearings, but the attacker was closing in fast, ready to strike again. Suddenly, a stern, authoritative voice shouted out and echoed through the concrete structure. "Hey! You! Stop right there!"

Frankie's blurred vision came into focus, and he observed a well-built security guard marching assertively toward the dangerous scene. Before the guard even had a chance to reach for his radio to call in the incident, the attacker swung his axe and severed the man's hand in one clean cut.

Blood gushed out of the stump, and the guard stepped back in total shock. He let out a screech of pain while the attacker stepped forward to deliver more agony. The villain lowered his weapon and aimed its long spike at the guard's torso. With malevolent force, he jammed the spike into the man's trunk repeatedly until he slumped down to the cool garage floor in a pool of his own blood.

With the attacker's focus fixed on the vulnerable guard, Frankie used this opportunity to sneak off and hide under a Subaru Outback parked across the garage. With blood now running from his mouth, the impaled guard could only watch weakly as the attacker raised his axe and came down on him powerfully with one of the blades. Chop after furious chop, the villain axed the guard into grisly pieces until what was left was unrecognizable.

Frankie was nowhere in sight—a revelation that the attacker came upon while catching his breath and composure, following the unplanned slaughter of the security guard. The villain peered around before looking over at Poe, who shook his head cluelessly. The mascot then faced a different direction and raised his wings, gesturing *What do we do now?* to a cohort who may have been watching things unfold from afar. Receiving no further instructions, the raven looked to the attacker and shrugged.

Slowly, with a methodical caution, the attacker gripped his weapon tightly and walked softly through the garage, inspecting any and all spots in which the escapee could have hidden. Soon, he caught sight of some spatters of blood that led in the direction of the Outback—one of only three vehicles parked in this isolated row of the garage.

Still reeling in pain from the axe hit, Frankie bit his lip and held his breath to stifle any whimpers or groans. In a taunting fashion, the villain dropped the head of the axe down to the floor and dragged one of the blades along as he circled all three vehicles. Frankie squeezed his eyes closed while the blood-curdling screeches of metal scraping concrete cut through the threatening silence.

The attacker kicked the first two cars, filling the garage with thunderous thumps that made Frankie flinch nervously. The sadistic villain then swung his axe under each of the two vehicles.

The quarterback's heart pounded a mile a minute, and his mind hurried to figure out what to do, where to go. Finally, the attacker sauntered slowly to the Outback before stopping and holding still for a few seconds that felt like a few lifetimes. As he did with the other two cars, he kicked the Outback and waited.

Frankie's eyes widened. It was now or never—4th and goal, five seconds left on the clock, the game on the line.

While standing there, the villain rhythmically tapped his weapon's spike onto the cement in a teasing manner.

Frankie trembled with anxiety, digging deep for some courage.

Suddenly, the quarterback lunged out and grabbed the enemy's ankles. Before the villain could raise his axe, Frankie tugged harder than he ever had in his life. The force yanked the evil man's ankles out from under him, sending him falling backward. On his way down, he cracked his head on a metal parking post.

Frankie wasted no time. Urgently, he slid out from under the Outback and straddled the attacker. A fire of vengeance raging inside of him, the quarterback dealt the enemy blow after blow to the face. When Frankie's hands were too gashed and bruised to continue, he tiredly rose to his feet and retrieved the enemy's axe. Summoning one last wind, the man raised the weapon and came down on the attacker, chop after chop, hacking him apart in gruesome style.

Poe backed up a few steps from his position, now concerned that he may be next in line to suffer this primal retaliation. Raw, unbridled rage in his eyes, Frankie glared at the mascot, ready to issue some more revenge. To his disbelief, a familiar voice came through P.A. speakers built into the confines of the garage.

"Frankie!... It's Walt."

The quarterback tried to compute what he had just heard, which snapped him out of his angry wrath, at least temporarily.

"Listen, Frankie... I want you to put that thing down and listen to me."

"Walt, what... what the hell's going on?"

"I only ever wanted you to be your best," said Walt. "It's a nasty business. You know that, kid. You can be on top one day, and in the gutter the next. Someone with your talent... it's a travesty to waste it.".

Frankie looked around, confused beyond measure.

Walt continued, "Too many distractions make a bad quarterback, Frankie. Lenore was a distraction. She didn't understand your gift, your mission, your responsibility to see your God-given talents through to the maximum levels of success. I had to do something about that."

"*Do something about that?* What the fuck are you saying to me, Walt?"

"And don't think I don't know about the Percocet and Stoli. Drugs and booze may get you through your daily demons for a bit, but ultimately, they make a loser of you on the football field. This exercise was originally intended to scare you, to put the fear of God in you, and get you back to caring about winning again. But... you let me down, kid. You're irredeemable, unfixable. We can't win a title with what you lack in your heart and mind. It hurts me to even say that, but we need to face where we're at here, son."

Tears streamed down Frankie's cheeks. Blistering fury and crushing sadness wrestled for dominance inside of him, but neither took complete hold.

"I've gotta let you go, pal. After this disaster of a season, we'll get a good pick in the first round of the draft. I'll recommend to Mr. Granderson and Lou that we take that QB from Florida State. *That* kid is a real winner, a born leader. I know *he* won't let me down," Walt said.

Frankie replied, "I sure hope he doesn't. Or he just might lose everything he ever loved. You lousy traitor bastard."

The injured, dejected quarterback dropped the axe and turned to leave, but it wasn't going to be that easy. Another masked attacker stood before him, holding out a speared rod that pierced him right through the heart. Frankie glanced at his bleeding impalement and then at the masked face of his executioner. Within seconds, he was dead. His body slumped, and the attacker pulled the spear from out of his chest.

The next morning, Frankie's car was found in a ravine, his battered corpse twisted behind the wheel. There were bottles of vodka and vials of painkillers recovered from inside the wreck. The Ravens wore memorial patches on their uniforms the rest of that miserable season, honoring what their quarterback gave of himself to win, and pondering what could have been if he had made it through the night.

THE END

Want More?

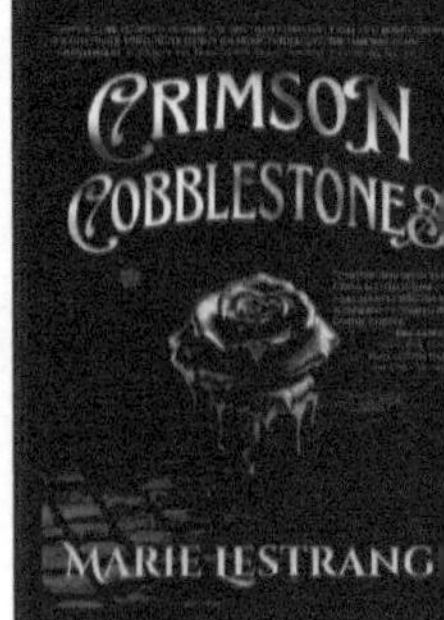